Weekly Reader Presents

The Legend of the Doozer Who Didn't

By Louise Gikow · Pictures by Barbara McClintock

Muppet Press
Henry Holt and Company
NEW YORK

Published by Henry Holt and Company,
521 Fifth Avenue, New York, New York 10175

Library of Congress Cataloging in Publication Data
Gikow, Louise.
The legend of the Doozer who didn't.
Summary: This "old legend" explains what happened to
one Doozer who violated Doozer tradition by stopping
working and going to school.
[1. Stories in rhyme. 2. Puppets—Fiction. 3. Work—
Fiction] I. McClintock, Barbara, ill. II. Title.
PZ8.3.G376Le 1984   [E]   84-6623
ISBN: 0-03-000717-8

Printed in the United States of America

ISBN 0-03-000717-8

This book is a presentation of
Weekly Reader Books

Weekly Reader Books offers book clubs for children
from preschool through high school.

For further information write to:
Weekly Reader Books
4343 Equity Drive
Columbus, Ohio 43228

The Legend
of the Doozer Who Didn't

IN old Doozer legends that old Doozers know,
A Doozer supposedly lived long ago.
They called him the Doozer Who Didn't, I'm told,
And if he were here, he'd be older than old.

When the Doozer Who Didn't was still very small
No one could guess he was different at all.
He played with his friends in the Radish Dust Glen
Building radish dust castles and radish dust men.

He was nice and quite bright, and his parents could see
That he seemed to be all that a Doozer could be.
He worked just as hard as he could while in school
And carefully studied the First Doozer Rule:

Building is good! Working is right!
Work is what makes every Doozer heart light!

Nobody knows why the trouble first started.
(This story is not for the weak or fainthearted.)
When awakened one morning, he stretched and he said,
"I think that I'd rather just stay here in bed."

"You're sick!" said his mother, suspecting a fever.
"I'm fine!" said the Doozer, not wanting to grieve her.
"I've never felt better! I'm fit as can be!
I just feel like doing…well…nothing. You see?"

His mother could *not* see, for she was aware
That school was beginning and he should be there.
She called in his father, who frowned and looked stern.
"Now, son," he said firmly, "you simply *must* learn."

"*Why* must I learn?" the small Doozer inquired.
"I'm late," said his father. "And I could be fired.
So get out of bed and head out like you should.
I'll explain it at dinner. Good-bye, and be good!"

So the Doozer Who Didn't got up, I believe.
He washed and he dressed and got ready to leave.

But he quietly said as he went out the door,
"I don't understand what this working is *for*."

The next sign of trouble occurred when he'd grown.
He was on the first shift. The noon whistle had blown.
He ate all his lunch. He was then heard to say,
"I don't think I'll work for the rest of the day."

The Doozers could barely believe their own ears.
Stop working? Why, no one had done it in years!
In fact no one *ever* had stopped that they knew.
It simply was *not* what a Doozer should do.

Not work? It's unheard of! It just isn't done!
All Doozers keep busy! For them, work is fun!
After all, that's the first thing they learn while in school—
It's right at the heart of the First Doozer Rule:

Working is good! Building's okay!
Doozers would much rather work hard than play!

The Doozer Who Didn't just couldn't care less.
He just simply liked to do nothing, I guess.
And when he stopped working, he started to *sing!*
And no matter who asked, he would not do a thing!

While he sang songs, he made up silly games
Like Filling the Helmets and Naming the Names
(In which he named all of the names that he knew.
As fast as he could. When he stopped, he was through.)

Wing nut
Girder
Auger
Scoop
Tweezer
Ratchet
Cantilever
Flange
Trowel
Wrench
Bolt
C-clamp
Clamp
Piper
Socket
Crane
Modem
Turbo
Toggle bolt
Plug
Lag bolt
Hammer
Bits
Stapler

But then, says the tale, as he sat and he sat,
The Doozer began to grow terribly *fat*.
He grew bigger and bigger and bigger in size
(Since he wasn't getting enough exercise!)

And then (also due to extreme inactivity
And partially caused by his total passivity)
He began growing fur! And a tail! And so tall
That he hardly resembled a Doozer at all!

He was totally useless, and just in the way.
All he did was eat Doozer constructions all day.
And the legend goes on to explain what it can—
So it was, say the Doozers, that *Fraggles* began!

Well, anyway, that's what the Doozers all say—
That a Fraggle is born when a Doozer must play.
And all mother Doozers remember this rule
And warn all their children who won't go to school:

Schooling is good! Working is right!
So do all your homework, and study all night!
For if you stop working or building, you see,
You'll turn into Fraggles as quick as can be!